This book belongs to

. . . .

For my teachers who inspired me and
the friends and family who over the years
have supported me. You know who you are.

ISBN 978-1-84135-914-4

First published 2012

Published by Award Publications Limited,
The Old Riding School, The Welbeck Estate,
Worksop, Nottinghamshire, S80 3LR

www.awardpublications.co.uk

13 2

Printed in China

Also available:
Goose
Goose Goes to the Zoo
Happy Birthday, Goose!
Goose on the Farm
Goose Goes Shopping

Goose Goes to School

by Laura Wall

AWARD PUBLICATIONS LIMITED

Today Sophie is going to school.

But Goose can't come.

Mum says geese aren't allowed in school.

So Sophie packs her bag ready to go.

Sophie and Mum walk to school.

"Goodbye, Goose!"

But on the way to school, Sophie thinks

she hears flappy footsteps behind her.

And when she gets to the playground ...

... she is sure she sees a familiar face.

But it can't be Goose, can it?

Mum said geese don't go to school.

Sophie goes into class and finds her chair.

Sophie's first lesson is the alphabet.

She tries to listen,
but she wishes Goose was with her.

But wait. What's that?

The children start to giggle.

G is for...

And the teacher gets cross.

But when she turns around,
she doesn't see Goose.

When the bell rings,
everyone runs outside to play.

Sophie and Goose play games.

Soon, the other children want to play
with Sophie and Goose, too.

Playtime is so much fun with Goose.

At the end of playtime ...

... Sophie goes back to class.

And Goose flaps off to play on the swings ...

... and wait until school is over.

That afternoon everyone paints a picture.

The teacher is very pleased
with their paintings.

And she decorates the classroom wall.

At hometime Sophie waits for Mum

with her new friends.

They ask if Goose will be back
again tomorrow.

"What do you think, Goose?"

"Honk!" says Goose.